THE BOXCAR CHILDREN MYSTERIES

THE BOXCAR CHILDREN
SURPRISE ISLAND
THE YELLOW HOUSE MYSTERY
MYSTERY RANCH
MIKE'S MYSTERY
BLUE BAY MYSTERY
THE WOODSHED MYSTERY
THE LIGHTHOUSE MYSTERY
MOUNTAIN TOP MYSTERY
SCHOOLHOUSE MYSTERY
CABOOSE MYSTERY
HOUSEBOAT MYSTERY
SNOWBOUND MYSTERY
TREE HOUSE MYSTERY
BICYCLE MYSTERY
MYSTERY IN THE SAND
MYSTERY BEHIND THE WALL
BUS STATION MYSTERY
BENNY UNCOVERS A MYSTERY
THE HAUNTED CABIN MYSTERY
THE DESERTED LIBRARY MYSTERY
THE ANIMAL SHELTER MYSTERY
THE OLD MOTEL MYSTERY
THE MYSTERY OF THE HIDDEN PAINTING
THE AMUSEMENT PARK MYSTERY
THE MYSTERY OF THE MIXED-UP ZOO
THE CAMP-OUT MYSTERY
THE MYSTERY GIRL
THE MYSTERY CRUISE
THE DISAPPEARING FRIEND MYSTERY
THE MYSTERY OF THE SINGING GHOST
THE MYSTERY IN THE SNOW
THE PIZZA MYSTERY
THE MYSTERY HORSE
THE MYSTERY AT THE DOG SHOW
THE CASTLE MYSTERY
THE MYSTERY OF THE LOST VILLAGE
THE MYSTERY ON THE ICE
THE MYSTERY OF THE PURPLE POOL
THE GHOST SHIP MYSTERY
THE MYSTERY IN WASHINGTON, DC
THE CANOE TRIP MYSTERY
THE MYSTERY OF THE HIDDEN BEACH
THE MYSTERY OF THE MISSING CAT
THE MYSTERY AT SNOWFLAKE INN

THE MYSTERY ON STAGE
THE DINOSAUR MYSTERY
THE MYSTERY OF THE STOLEN MUSIC
THE MYSTERY AT THE BALL PARK
THE CHOCOLATE SUNDAE MYSTERY
THE MYSTERY OF THE HOT AIR BALLOON
THE MYSTERY BOOKSTORE
THE PILGRIM VILLAGE MYSTERY
THE MYSTERY OF THE STOLEN BOXCAR
THE MYSTERY IN THE CAVE
THE MYSTERY ON THE TRAIN
THE MYSTERY AT THE FAIR
THE MYSTERY OF THE LOST MINE
THE GUIDE DOG MYSTERY
THE HURRICANE MYSTERY
THE PET SHOP MYSTERY
THE MYSTERY OF THE SECRET MESSAGE
THE FIREHOUSE MYSTERY
THE MYSTERY IN SAN FRANCISCO
THE NIAGARA FALLS MYSTERY
THE MYSTERY AT THE ALAMO
THE OUTER SPACE MYSTERY
THE SOCCER MYSTERY
THE MYSTERY IN THE OLD ATTIC
THE GROWLING BEAR MYSTERY
THE MYSTERY OF THE LAKE MONSTER
THE MYSTERY AT PEACOCK HALL
THE WINDY CITY MYSTERY
THE BLACK PEARL MYSTERY
THE CEREAL BOX MYSTERY
THE PANTHER MYSTERY
THE MYSTERY OF THE QUEEN'S JEWELS
THE STOLEN SWORD MYSTERY
THE BASKETBALL MYSTERY
THE MOVIE STAR MYSTERY
THE MYSTERY OF THE PIRATE'S MAP
THE GHOST TOWN MYSTERY
THE MYSTERY OF THE BLACK RAVEN
THE MYSTERY IN THE MALL
THE MYSTERY IN NEW YORK
THE GYMNASTICS MYSTERY
THE POISON FROG MYSTERY
THE MYSTERY OF THE EMPTY SAFE
THE HOME RUN MYSTERY
THE GREAT BICYCLE RACE MYSTERY

THE MYSTERY OF THE WILD PONIES
THE MYSTERY IN THE COMPUTER GAME
THE HONEYBEE MYSTERY
THE MYSTERY AT THE CROOKED HOUSE
THE HOCKEY MYSTERY
THE MYSTERY OF THE MIDNIGHT DOG
THE MYSTERY OF THE SCREECH OWL
THE SUMMER CAMP MYSTERY
THE COPYCAT MYSTERY
THE HAUNTED CLOCK TOWER MYSTERY
THE MYSTERY OF THE TIGER'S EYE
THE DISAPPEARING STAIRCASE MYSTERY
THE MYSTERY ON BLIZZARD MOUNTAIN
THE MYSTERY OF THE SPIDER'S CLUE
THE CANDY FACTORY MYSTERY
THE MYSTERY OF THE MUMMY'S CURSE
THE MYSTERY OF THE STAR RUBY
THE STUFFED BEAR MYSTERY
THE MYSTERY OF ALLIGATOR SWAMP
THE MYSTERY AT SKELETON POINT
THE TATTLETALE MYSTERY
THE COMIC BOOK MYSTERY
THE GREAT SHARK MYSTERY
THE ICE CREAM MYSTERY
THE MIDNIGHT MYSTERY
THE MYSTERY IN THE FORTUNE COOKIE
THE BLACK WIDOW SPIDER MYSTERY
THE RADIO MYSTERY
THE MYSTERY OF THE RUNAWAY GHOST
THE FINDERS KEEPERS MYSTERY
THE MYSTERY OF THE HAUNTED BOXCAR
THE CLUE IN THE CORN MAZE
THE GHOST OF THE CHATTERING BONES
THE SWORD OF THE SILVER KNIGHT
THE GAME STORE MYSTERY
THE MYSTERY OF THE ORPHAN TRAIN
THE VANISHING PASSENGER
THE GIANT YO-YO MYSTERY
THE CREATURE IN OGOPOGO LAKE
THE ROCK 'N' ROLL MYSTERY
THE SECRET OF THE MASK
THE SEATTLE PUZZLE
THE GHOST IN THE FIRST ROW
THE BOX THAT WATCH FOUND
A HORSE NAMED DRAGON

THE GREAT DETECTIVE RACE
THE GHOST AT THE DRIVE-IN MOVIE
THE MYSTERY OF THE TRAVELING TOMATOES
THE SPY GAME
THE DOG-GONE MYSTERY
THE VAMPIRE MYSTERY
SUPERSTAR WATCH
THE SPY IN THE BLEACHERS
THE AMAZING MYSTERY SHOW
THE PUMPKIN HEAD MYSTERY
THE CUPCAKE CAPER
THE CLUE IN THE RECYCLING BIN
MONKEY TROUBLE
THE ZOMBIE PROJECT
THE GREAT TURKEY HEIST
THE GARDEN THIEF
THE BOARDWALK MYSTERY
THE MYSTERY OF THE FALLEN TREASURE
THE RETURN OF THE GRAVEYARD GHOST
THE MYSTERY OF THE STOLEN SNOWBOARD
THE MYSTERY OF THE WILD WEST BANDIT
THE MYSTERY OF THE SOCCER SNITCH
THE MYSTERY OF THE GRINNING GARGOYLE
THE MYSTERY OF THE MISSING POP IDOL
THE MYSTERY OF THE STOLEN DINOSAUR BONES
THE MYSTERY AT THE CALGARY STAMPEDE
THE SLEEPY HOLLOW MYSTERY
THE LEGEND OF THE IRISH CASTLE
THE CELEBRITY CAT CAPER
HIDDEN IN THE HAUNTED SCHOOL
THE ELECTION DAY DILEMMA
JOURNEY ON A RUNAWAY TRAIN
THE CLUE IN THE PAPYRUS SCROLL
THE DETOUR OF THE ELEPHANTS
THE SHACKLETON SABOTAGE
THE KHIPU AND THE FINAL KEY
THE DOUGHNUT WHODUNIT
THE ROBOT RANSOM
THE LEGEND OF THE HOWLING WEREWOLF
THE DAY OF THE DEAD MYSTERY
THE HUNDRED-YEAR MYSTERY
THE SEA TURTLE MYSTERY
NEW! SECRET ON THE THIRTEENTH FLOOR
NEW! THE POWER DOWN MYSTERY

THE BOXCAR CHILDREN®

CREATED BY
GERTRUDE CHANDLER WARNER

BOOK

153

THE POWER DOWN MYSTERY

ILLUSTRATED BY
ANTHONY VanARSDALE

ALBERT WHITMAN & COMPANY
CHICAGO, ILLINOIS

Printed in the United States of America
10 9 8 7 6 5 4 3 2 1 LB 24 23 22 21 20 19

Illustrations by Anthony VanArsdale

Visit the Boxcar Children online at www.boxcarchildren.com.
For more information about Albert Whitman & Company,
visit our website at www.albertwhitman.com.

100 years of Albert Whitman & Company
Celebrate with us in 2019!

Contents

1. The Coming Storm   1

2. Unplugged   12

3. The Bear Facts   24

4. Shipwreck on Main   33

5. Follow That Bear!   42

6. Copies and Clues   53

7. Getting Warmer, Getting Cooler   65

8. The Bear Trap   76

9. Treasure on a Trailer   87

10. Cleaning Up Clues   97

The Coming Storm

The Aldens stood on the boardwalk and looked out over the harbor. Grandfather had brought the children to Port Elizabeth for the annual tall ships festival. But now the ships were sailing away.

Six-year-old Benny swung underneath the wooden railing at the edge of the marina. "Look at all the sails on that one!" he said. "Ten sails. No, eleven. Wait, twelve!"

At first, he had been sad the festival was ending early. But seeing the big boats in action was exciting. Colorful sails billowed on tall wooden masts. And the old-fashioned ships crashed through the waves.

In the marina, waves lapped onto the docks.

The Power Down Mystery

With the tall ships gone, most of the docks were empty. On the ones that weren't, people scrambled about, getting ready to move newer, smaller boats.

Henry leaned his elbows on the railing next to Benny. Unlike his brother, Henry wasn't watching the ships. He was looking at the dark clouds chasing them away. At fourteen, Henry was the oldest of the Alden children, and he liked to pay attention to the weather. "The storm is coming in fast," he said. "I hope everyone gets to safety."

"The real storm isn't supposed to hit until later tonight," said Grandfather. "The ships will have plenty of time to find shelter up the coast."

"I'm glad we have people to forecast the weather," ten-year-old Violet said. "Imagine if we didn't have any warning before the storm."

Grandfather's friend Marie Freeman spoke up. "There are ships at the bottom of this harbor from the days when the sailors didn't get enough warning before storms hit." Ms. Freeman was the Aldens' host for the festival. She had lived in Port Elizabeth all her life. She loved to study old things.

"Even today, weather can be hard to predict,"

said Grandfather. "But it seems pretty likely that this storm will reach us before it dies out. I think the folks who run the festival made the right decision."

Benny was still more interested in the ships than the storm. As the children started walking toward the exit of the marina, he asked, "How do they know where to go? Once they get away from shore, all there is is waves! They don't even have street signs to follow! Don't they get lost?"

Ms. Freeman smiled. "I have a feeling those big, old ships might have some new technology onboard to tell them where they are. But sailors still have to know how to travel the old-fashioned way, just in case. What would they do if their computers failed?"

Benny stopped suddenly. "In the middle of the ocean? They'd never get home!"

"They would if they had the old tools and knew how to use them," Henry said. "We should try using a compass and map to find our way around."

"That sounds fun," Jessie said.

The Aldens came to the end of the marina. Violet noticed a line of smaller, newer-looking boats. Instead of sailing the boats away, people were loading them onto big trailers. On the dock next to the boats was a thin man in an orange raincoat. Around him were half a dozen people. They looked to be arguing with him.

"That's Hector Valencia," said Ms. Freeman. "He owns this marina. Poor guy. Ending the festival early can't be good for his business."

"Those people don't look happy with him," said Henry.

"I suppose everyone is trying to get their boats out of the water before the storm rolls in," said Grandfather. "But it looks like there's some sort of holdup."

"Looks like the boats are being inspected," Ms. Freeman said. "Unfortunately, there are rumors of smugglers here in Port Elizabeth."

Benny's eyes got big. "Smugglers? You mean like pirates?"

Ms. Freeman chuckled. "Not exactly. Smugglers are people who bring things in or out of the country illegally."

"What happens if they get caught?" Violet asked.

"It depends," said Ms. Freeman. "Say the

smugglers brought in something that was legal to own, like jewels, but they snuck it in without paying taxes. They'd probably get a fine."

"That seems silly," said Jessie. "Why risk a fine when you could be honest and not get in trouble?"

Ms. Freeman smiled. "That is a very good question. Sadly, not everyone is as sensible as you are. Most people are honest though. They just want to get their boats to safety."

Henry pointed at a large speedboat out in the bay. "I wonder whose boat that is," he said. The boat was anchored, and it didn't look like there was anyone aboard.

"I hope the owner hasn't forgotten about it," said Jessie. "If they don't move it and the storm hits, who knows what could happen to it?"

The empty boat bobbing on the dark water gave Benny a bad feeling. It reminded him of spooky stories he'd heard about ghost ships and pirates. He was happy when Ms. Freeman changed the subject.

"I'd like to check in on my shop before the storm hits," Ms. Freeman said. "Would you all mind if we stopped by?"

The Aldens agreed, and they followed Ms. Freeman into town. Along Main Street, they passed by empty gift shops and restaurants. Many were boarded up to protect against the coming storm.

The Happy Bear Ice-Cream Shop was just off Main Street. Outside the shop there was a tall statue of a bear standing up on its back legs. The bear was wearing blue overalls and holding an ice-cream cone piled high with scoops.

"You didn't tell us you had an ice-cream shop!" said Benny.

"I love your statue," said Violet. "It goes perfectly with the name of your shop."

"Why, thank you," said Ms. Freeman. "Bears became the symbol for our town a few years ago, and this fellow was made for my shop. I liked him so much, I changed the shop's name to match."

"So it's a town mascot?" Jessie asked.

"That's right," Ms. Freeman said. "The tourists like taking pictures with all the different bear statues around town."

A man in front of the shop next door gave a snort. "Maybe the storm will do everyone a favor

6

and blow that one away."

"Why do you say that?" Henry asked.

The man stopped hammering and wiped his brow. He spoke with a strong southern accent. "I believe this should be a high-class town with high-class shops. People see that silly bear and the silly name and think they can bring their drippity ice cream anyplace." He frowned at the children. "Kids come into my shop and let it drip all over. Then they touch things with their sticky hands."

The man turned back to his work. "At least my shop will be protected from this coming storm," he said.

Once the Aldens were in the ice-cream shop, Violet whispered, "That man didn't seem very nice."

Ms. Freeman sighed. "That is George Williams. He's not really so bad. He just moved here from Georgia. He doesn't understand Port Elizabeth yet. If he had it his way, there'd only be fancy gift shops like his."

"Why does he want you to change your shop's name?" asked Jessie.

"Yeah, I like The Happy Bear," said Benny. "It's... happy!"

Ms. Freeman gave a small smile. "My shop used to be called Sailor's Delight Sweets and Treats. It went along with the name of the shop next door, The Stylish Sailor Boutique. But a couple years ago, I decided to just sell ice cream and changed the name. He's always trying to get me to go back to selling fancy candies and knickknacks."

"Well, I think ice cream is the perfect thing to sell," said Benny. "Shoppers need energy. They can take a break with ice cream and have more energy to shop."

"I'll bet you're right," Ms. Freeman said. "How about some energy for you kids? Give your orders to Savannah."

The young woman behind the counter had not looked up from her cell phone since the Aldens entered the shop.

Ms. Freeman sighed. "Savannah!"

The young woman jumped and looked up. She had long, brown hair and wore a purple shirt.

"Take the Aldens' orders, please," Ms. Freeman

said. "I'm going to check on the generator."

As the woman rang them up, Violet said, "I like your shirt. Purple is my favorite color. Your bracelets and earrings are nice too. Are the red stones rubies? And pearls?"

The young woman blushed. "Oh, these? They aren't anything special. Only stuff I put together." She turned away to scoop ice cream. Violet wanted to ask about her name tag, which said *Sarah* instead of Savannah. But it did not seem like the woman wanted to talk.

The children and Grandfather sat at a table and ate their ice cream. Soon Ms. Freeman joined them.

Henry asked, "Are you worried about the storm, Ms. Freeman? Should we put up boards like the man next door?"

"I've seen enough storms hit Port Elizabeth," Ms. Freeman said. "We'll survive one more. I'm only concerned about one thing. We've had some issues with the power lately. It's the strangest thing. Some days I come in, and the ice cream is soft and runny—like it's been melting overnight."

"That is strange," Henry said.

"I have a backup generator though," Ms. Freeman continued. "So if the power does go out, the generator will turn on. It will keep the ice cream cold and run the security system."

Benny's eyes got wide. "Security system? Do you think someone will come and steal the ice cream?"

Ms. Freeman smiled. "More likely they'd steal money from the cash register. We don't keep much overnight, but it's better to be safe. Things can get a little crazy when a storm hits. You never know what people will do."

"Maybe we should stay here and protect the ice cream," said Benny. "Just in case."

Everyone laughed. "We'll be more comfortable at Ms. Freeman's house," said Grandfather. He winked at Benny. "We can get some ice cream to go, for after dinner."

Benny nodded. "That's a good idea. And after the storm, we'll come back and make sure the ice cream is safe."

CHAPTER 2

Unplugged

The wind blew hard all night. Rain drummed the roof and washed down the windows.

In the morning, the power was out. Everyone gathered in the kitchen. As Violet peered out the window, she thought back to the children's first night in the boxcar.

After their parents died, Henry, Jessie, Violet, and Benny had run away. A bad storm hit, and they had no place to stay. Then they found an old boxcar in the woods. It had rained and rained, but no water came in. The boxcar was such a good shelter the children made it their home. That was where Grandfather found them. At first, Violet and her siblings had been afraid Grandfather would be mean, but they realized he wasn't mean at all. He gave them a real home in Greenfield, Connecticut. He even moved the boxcar to their backyard to use as a clubhouse.

Henry looked over Violet's shoulder. "I don't see lights on anywhere. Maybe the whole area lost power."

"Probably," said Ms. Freeman. "After a storm like that, we might not have power for days."

Violet turned from the window. "Mrs. McGregor will be worried. We should call and tell her we're okay." Mrs. McGregor was the Aldens' housekeeper. She was back in Greenfield with their dog, Watch.

"I'm worried!" said Benny. "With no power, what will we make to eat?"

"We can eat cold food, Benny," said Jessie.

Benny nodded. "But will the food in the refrigerator go bad?" he asked. "We should eat the rest of the ice cream before it melts!"

Grandfather ruffled Benny's hair. "We can find a healthier breakfast. Let me call Mrs. McGregor first." He pulled out his cell phone. "Uh-oh. I can't get a connection."

"Without power, the cell phone towers don't work," said Ms. Freeman. "A few have battery backups, but they run out quickly when many people use them after a storm."

Violet looked at Grandfather. "What are we going to do? I don't want Mrs. McGregor to wonder if we are okay."

"Not to worry," said Ms. Freeman. "We'll just have to do things the old-fashioned way."

She went into the next room and brought back a big telephone with a spinning dial and a long cord. "I still have a landline," she explained. "The wires go underground, so they are protected from storms. This phone might look old, but it almost always works when the power goes out."

Ms. Freeman showed Violet how to use the spinning dial on the phone, and Violet called Mrs. McGregor and told her everyone was okay. "It's strange not having power," Violet added. "We can't use our computers or the TV. But we'll take care of ourselves." She passed the phone to Grandfather.

Ms. Freeman put another object on the table,

and the children gathered around. The thing looked like a plastic clock with a handle on top.

"What's that?" Benny asked.

"A hand-crank radio," Ms. Freeman said. She pointed at a black arm attached to the radio. "That is the crank."

"What does it do?" asked Benny.

"Turning the crank charges a battery inside," Ms. Freeman said. "After a few minutes, you'll get an hour of power."

"Cool!" Benny held the radio and turned the crank.

"Now we can listen to music," said Jessie.

"And get news," Ms. Freeman said. "This is a weather alert radio. It will tell us about any emergencies."

"You really know how to prepare for a storm," Henry said.

Ms. Freeman nodded. "I have an emergency supply bag. It has a first aid kit, two flashlights, batteries, and a whistle to call for help. I keep packaged foods in the pantry and drinking water in sealed jugs in case something happens to the water supply."

Benny put down the crank radio. "My arm is getting tired. I need breakfast!"

"It's your lucky day, Mr. Benny," said Ms. Freeman. "We need to eat a lot of food."

Benny bounced in his seat. "Really?"

Ms. Freeman nodded. "Without power, the fridge is getting warmer. Things will start to spoil. We should eat what we can before it goes bad."

Jessie tapped her chin. "We shouldn't open the door for very long," she said. "The closed door helps keep in the cold. Why don't you tell me what you want, and I'll get it."

"Let's see," said Ms. Freeman. "Grab the eggs, milk, and cheese."

Jessie opened the refrigerator. She quickly passed the food to Violet, who put it on the counter.

"Get the hash browns from the freezer," Ms. Freeman said. Those joined the pile near the stove.

"You can cook without electricity?" Benny asked.

"You sure can." Ms. Freeman lit a match, turned a knob on the stove, and held the match to a burner. A circle of flames lit up. "It's a gas stove. It usually uses electricity to light the gas, but a match works just as well."

Ms. Freeman cooked omelets. She made coffee in a pot that brewed on the stove. Jessie poured milk while Violet set the table. Henry cranked the radio to build up its power. Then they all sat down to a big breakfast.

A few minutes later, Grandfather patted his stomach. "That was delicious. I'm stuffed."

"The freezer is still almost full," said Jessie. "We won't be able to eat everything today."

"We can try!" said Benny. "We don't want to waste good food, remember?"

Ms. Freeman laughed. "I'll show you a trick." She got a penny from her purse. "This will let us know if the food stays good. Can you guess how?"

The children all thought for a bit. Finally, Violet asked, "Is this a riddle?"

"Maybe it's a mystery," said Benny. "We like mysteries!"

"It's more of a handy little trick," said Ms. Freeman. "I'll give you a hint. If the power is out for a long time, the food in the freezer will melt. How do you know if that has happened?"

"The frozen food will be soft," said Henry.

"Or, if you have ice cubes in trays," said Jessie, "the ice will become water."

Ms. Freeman nodded. "When the power goes back on, the freezer will get cold again. Something might thaw and go bad, then freeze again."

Jessie frowned. "You wouldn't know. The ice cubes would refreeze. The food would get hard again."

"Right." Ms. Freeman opened the freezer and put the penny on a cube in the ice tray. "The ice cubes are hard, so the penny sits on top. If the ice thaws, the penny will sink. And if the ice cubes freeze again, the penny will stay on the bottom."

Jessie grinned. "I get it. If the penny is on top of the ice, the food is still good. If the penny has sunk, the food might have gone bad."

"That's a neat trick," Henry said. He carried their dishes to the sink. "What are we going to do today, after we clean up? We can't visit the tall ships festival anymore."

Violet looked out the window. "It's still raining

hard. I guess we won't play outside."

"We can't watch TV or use computers," Jessie said. "Ms. Freeman, do you have board games?"

"A few," she said. "And if you'd like to try a compass, I have one."

"Yes, please," Henry said. "We can practice navigating like the ships at sea."

The Aldens kept busy all day long. Henry taught Benny to use the compass. The children played board games. Grandfather taught them to play charades, and each of them took turns trying to act out a word without speaking. The rest of the group tried to guess the word, which usually led to lots of laughter. They ate food from the freezer and refrigerator, starting with the items that would go bad first. After dinner, they each had a bowl of ice cream.

In the evening, Ms. Freeman said, "It looks like the weather is finally starting to clear up. I wonder if there's any news. Turn up the radio, please."

Henry adjusted the dials on the radio, and everyone listened. A report came on. "The tropical storm weakened as it moved up the coast," a man

said. "However, we have reports of flooding and wind damage in Port Elizabeth. Residents should stay indoors until the storm lets up."

"Well, there's nothing we can do tonight," Ms. Freeman said. "We'll have to wait till morning to check on the shop."

After the sun went down, the children found it easy to go to bed early. In the morning, they woke to bright sunshine pouring in their windows. The power was still out, but the storm had passed. Reports on the weather radio said that floodwater in town had started to recede.

After breakfast, the Aldens rode in Ms. Freeman's pickup truck into town. Jessie helped Benny follow along using the compass and a map. As they got closer to town, they passed by several downed trees. There were also places where the drains were clogged, and deep puddles covered the street. At one point the water was too deep to go through.

"Where to, navigator?" Ms. Freeman asked Benny.

Benny scrunched up his face and whispered

something to Jessie, who nodded. "Take a left!" he said to Ms. Freeman.

"See, Benny? It isn't so hard to find your way the old-fashioned way," said Grandfather.

"At least not with street signs!" said Benny.

Before long, Ms. Freeman pulled up outside The Happy Bear Ice-Cream Shop. "The roof looks okay," she said. "No broken windows."

"Something's different..." said Henry, but he could not tell what.

It was Jessie who figured it out. "The happy bear..." she said. "It's gone!"

Ms. Freeman hurried into the store to make sure nothing else was missing. She flipped a light switch back and forth. "The power is out! What happened to the generator?" She rushed to the back of the shop.

Benny went to the ice-cream case and frowned. "My double-chocolate ice cream is double-chocolate soup!"

The Aldens joined Ms. Freeman in the back alley. She stood in front of a silver metal box, which must have held the generator. "I don't understand what went wrong!" she said.

Jessie tried to see past her. "Did the storm damage it?"

"It must have." Ms. Freeman opened the door to the generator. "I can't see anything wrong though."

"Wait a minute." Jessie moved in closer. "The lock on the door is broken!"

The Aldens looked at one another. Henry said, "Storms might cause damage, but they don't break locks."

CHAPTER

The Bear Facts

"Let's look for clues," said Jessie. "If someone shut down the power to the shop, there must be a reason."

Grandfather and Ms. Freeman stayed in back to look at the generator. Henry and Violet went in front of the shop to look for clues about the bear. Jessie and Benny searched inside.

After a while, the children went over what they had found.

"The only thing wrong in the shop is the melted ice cream in the display case," said Jessie.

Benny pressed his face against the glass. "It's very sad."

"We didn't find much either," said Henry. "But

it does look like there was some flooding on the street outside. The water left behind lots of sticks and dirt."

"That makes sense," said Jessie. "The radio did say there was flooding, and that the water had receded."

"Well," said Grandfather, coming back into the shop. "We can't seem to find anything wrong the generator."

"I'm afraid to touch the thing," said Ms. Freeman. "I don't want to make things worse. I need an electrician, but I'm sure they are all busy today." She looked at her watch. "Where's Sarah? We should have opened twenty minutes ago."

Ms. Freeman's words reminded Violet of something. Ms. Freeman had called her employee Savannah when they first were in the shop, but the girl's name tag had said *Sarah*. "I'm confused," said Violet. "Is her name Sarah or Savannah?"

Ms. Freeman explained. "Her real name is Sarah Pierce, but Savannah is what she answers to. It's the name she uses for her online store."

Benny tilted his head. "Why doesn't she just use

25

one name? Having two names sounds confusing."

"I suppose Savan—er...Sarah, thinks that *Savannah* sounds better for selling her jewelry," said Ms. Freeman. "That's what her online store sells—homemade jewelry. I admire how much work she puts into it, as long as it doesn't affect her work here. And normally it doesn't. She's usually the first to arrive and the last to leave."

"Maybe she thought the shop wouldn't be open today," said Jessie. "If she doesn't have a landline, she couldn't call you to find out."

"That's true," said Ms. Freeman. "Mr. Williams is opening his store next door. I'll tell him about the generator. It powers both our shops."

The children followed her outside. Ms. Freeman explained to Mr. Williams what had happened with the generator.

Mr. Williams spoke in his southern accent. "The power outage doesn't hurt me. Nothing in my shop will melt. If losing power for a day or two is the price I pay for not seeing that bear again, that's fine by me." He opened his door and glanced back at Ms. Freeman. "Sorry about your ice cream," he said as he went inside.

Benny crossed his arms. "He didn't sound sorry."

"He really didn't like the bear," said Ms. Freeman, leading the way back into her shop. "And he doesn't care much for my ice cream either. He's always complaining about people getting runny ice cream on his floor. Speaking of which, I'd better dump out the ice cream in that case."

"Can't you freeze it again?" Benny asked.

Ms. Freeman shook her head. "Ice cream is made by churning—it works air into the cream. If it melts and freezes again, it will get grainy with larger ice crystals."

"It still might taste good," said Benny.

Ms. Freeman smiled at him. "I suppose so. But it might not be safe to eat. Bacteria can grow on warm dairy products. I wouldn't want to make anyone sick."

"We'll pour out the ice cream," said Henry. He went behind the counter and opened the back of the case. Jessie joined him. Together they lifted out a large tub of strawberry ice cream and poured pink soup into the sink.

Benny put his hands up to his face. "It hurts to watch!"

Ms. Freeman patted his shoulder. "Don't worry. I have more ice cream in the freezer." Then she sighed. "I only hope it stays cold. If it doesn't and I have to throw it out, I don't know what I'll do."

The Bear Facts

Violet thought about the broken lock on the generator door. "Do you think someone did this on purpose?" She didn't like to think anyone would be so mean. But George Williams had seemed pleased that Ms. Freeman's shop was in trouble. "Could Mr. Williams be trying to put you out of business?"

Ms. Freeman pulled out a chair and sat at one of the tables. "That would be one way for him to get a new neighbor, I suppose."

"Would he really go that far?" Grandfather asked.

Ms. Freeman shook her head. "George Williams might not like my shop. That doesn't mean he'd break our generator to put me out of business. And he couldn't have planned the storm."

Violet sat down at the table. "Maybe Mr. Williams wouldn't break the generator, but he might move the bear. He seemed happy that it was gone."

Ms. Freeman frowned. "I can't imagine I have two enemies. Surely the bear was simply washed away by the storm. That kind of thing happens."

Henry and Jessie joined them at the table. They needed to wait for the sink to drain before pouring in more ice cream.

"We should see what else the storm did," said Henry. "If it washed away other stuff around town, it might have taken the bear too."

Jessie pushed her hair out of her face. The air seemed damp after the storm. "You said the bear is a town mascot," she said. "How did that happen?"

Ms. Freeman leaned back with a smile. "It started two years ago. A really bad storm hit Port Elizabeth—worse than this one. Dozens of homes and businesses were destroyed."

"That's awful," said Henry.

"It was, at first," said Ms. Freeman. "But good things started happening. People started helping each other. Then one day, a black bear came to town. It walked right down Main Street, walking on two legs like a person."

"Were you scared?" asked Violet.

"No, I watched through that window right there." Ms. Freeman pointed to the front of the shop. "Most people knew to stay away. But people took videos. The bear looked funny walking on its back legs. People posted the videos online. Thousands of people watched those videos within a few days."

The Bear Facts

"The bear got famous!" said Benny.

"That's right," said Ms. Freeman. "Animal control got some bear experts here. They discovered the bear had hurt its front paws in the storm. That's why it walked on its back legs. They brought the bear in, and a vet fixed its paws."

"Thank goodness," said Jessie. "Do you think the bear came to town trying to get help?"

Ms. Freeman shrugged. "I don't know. In any case, once it had healed, the bear was released back into the wild. It became a symbol for the town. The bear got through a tough time and survived. So would we. People had stopped coming to town right after the storm. They thought everything would be closed. But then Port Elizabeth made the news with the bear. People got interested. More tourists came."

"They probably hoped they'd see the bear," said Jessie. "But it went back to the wild."

"Exactly," said Ms. Freeman. "We couldn't keep a live, wild bear in town. That wouldn't be fair to the bear, or safe for us. Instead, some local artists had the idea of making bear statues. The artists would have each bear wearing or holding something different."

"Like your bear's ice-cream cone," said Benny. "It tells people this is an ice-cream shop."

"I saw another bear holding a kite," Jessie said. "That was in front of a toy store."

"There must be twenty bears in town," Ms. Freeman said. "Each one is different." She sighed. "I sure did like that bear. Oh well, it's gone now." She turned aside, blinking away tears.

"Let's finish with the ice cream," Henry said. He motioned his brother and sisters to follow. Behind the counter, he whispered to them. "That statue meant a lot to Ms. Freeman. Maybe the storm didn't wash it out to sea. If so, we should find it for her."

"We're good at finding lost things!" said Benny.

Jessie smiled. "If we find it, it might give us a clue to what happened here."

Benny bounced on his toes. "Hooray! We have a mystery, and we get to help. I like mysteries and helping almost as much as I like ice cream."

4

Shipwreck on Main

The children finished pouring out the ice cream. They put the empty cardboard containers into the garbage out back. Then Henry said, "We'd like to look around town."

"I'd better stay here in case Sarah shows up," said Ms. Freeman. "I'm not sure how else to contact her."

"I'll wait with you, Marie," Grandfather said. "You children have fun, but be careful. The storm might have left debris in the streets. Watch your step, and don't touch any garbage without gloves on."

As the children walked down the street, Henry said, "If the storm washed away the bear, the water

33

might carry the statue toward the ocean. Let's head to the marina."

Benny looked at the map. And before long, he was leading them back to the marina.

"It should be a left turn here." But when Benny got to the corner, he stopped and said, "That's not on the map!"

As Henry, Jessie, and Violet got to the corner, they saw what he was talking about.

In the middle of Main Street, a large boat sat on its side, surrounded by a group of people.

"A real shipwreck!" said Benny, bouncing with excitement. "I bet there's hidden treasure inside!"

Jessie giggled. "What makes you think that?"

Benny stared at the boat with wide eyes. "Every shipwreck should have hidden treasure."

"I hope everyone is okay," said Henry. "Let's take a closer look."

The boat was not one of the tall ships from the festival. It looked like someone's private boat. The cabin roof was red. The rest of the boat looked white underneath the mud.

Jessie gasped. "That's the boat from the other

day! Henry pointed it out, remember? It was floating in the water by itself."

The Aldens joined the crowd around the boat. A woman said, "I have a trailer you can use. I'm not sure how we'll get the boat onto it though."

Someone else said, "You'll need a crane to lift that boat. You should have moved it yesterday."

The marina manager, Mr. Valencia, studied the boat and shook his head. "Where were you before the storm, Eric? Why didn't you take your boat out of the water?"

A stocky man with dark hair threw his arms into the air. "Leave me alone, why don't you? I don't need advice. I can take care of my own boat."

Jessie whispered to the others. "That must be the boat's owner. Mr. Valencia called him Eric."

"He's not very grateful about people wanting to help," said Violet.

Benny gasped. "Look!" He pointed at the boat.

The others studied the boat for a moment, but they did not see what Benny was talking about. "What are we looking at?" Henry asked.

"It's gone now. Someone was looking out of one

of those little windows. There's someone hiding inside..." Benny paused. He got a serious look on his face. "Or maybe it's a ghost ship!"

Henry smiled. "There's no such thing as ghost ships, Benny. The boat is partly filled with water. You can see it through the windows on the side of the boat. You probably just saw something floating in the water."

"It was a person!" said Benny. "They were bald with big, red earrings."

"Whatever it was, it's not there now," said Jessie. "Let's get a closer look."

As the Aldens moved toward the boat, the man named Eric hurried over. "What are you looking at?" he demanded.

Jessie gave him a friendly smile. "We've never seen a boat in the middle of the street before. I hope you can get it fixed and back in the water."

He waved her away. "Yeah, yeah, everyone is sorry. But I'm the one who has to deal with it." He turned away and then swung back. "You kids keep away from this boat! I don't want anyone on it."

"Of course not," said Henry. "We wouldn't do

anything so dangerous. The boat is on its side, and it might have been damaged by the storm. Besides, we wouldn't come aboard without permission."

"Right, that's it," said the man. "It's dangerous. Keep back." He stomped away.

Jessie frowned. "I don't think anyone is inside that boat. Still, that man acted very strange."

"He doesn't want us to find his hidden treasure," Benny said.

Henry laughed. "I just remembered something. In nautical terms, 'main' means the high seas. Like in that old song, 'Sailing, sailing, over the bounding main.' Instead of a shipwreck over the main seas, we got a shipwreck on Main Street."

"That's funny," said Violet. "Let's keep looking for the bear."

The children walked down Main Street toward the marina. On the way, they saw seaweed, branches, even big logs. And a lot of trash.

"Some of these things could have blown on the wind," said Violet. "The boat must weigh a lot. Did the wind push it into town?"

"I think I know what happened," said Henry. "You

know that normal tides go in and out each day."

"When the tide is out, we can walk on the beach," said Violet. "When the tide is high, it might cover the beach."

Henry nodded. "People build their houses well above the high-tide line. They wouldn't want to get flooded every time the tide comes in."

He pointed toward the marina, which wasn't far. "The water usually stays below the docks and the marina. During a tropical storm like a hurricane, the winds push more water to shore. It's called a storm surge. The sea level can rise a lot higher than usual. It might be fifteen or twenty feet higher than a regular high tide."

Jessie turned to look back at the boat. It was hard to believe the water rose so high it carried the boat up the street. "When the water went down, it left the boat behind," she said.

"Imagine leaving your boat in the ocean and finding it on Main Street," said Violet. "I feel bad for that man."

"I still think he's hiding something," said Benny.

"There's Hector Valencia up ahead," said Henry.

"Let's see what he knows." Henry called to the marina manager, who was headed back to the marina. The man waited for the children.

"Mr. Valencia," said Henry, "do you know why that man didn't move his boat yesterday?"

Mr. Valencia shook his head. "Everyone knew about the storm warning, including Eric Pruett. I don't know why he didn't take care of his boat."

"Maybe he didn't get the message," Violet said.

Mr. Valencia thought for a moment. "That can't be it," he said. "I saw him yesterday afternoon. I remember telling him that the officials needed to inspect all the boats. I warned him to be ready so he could leave as soon as they finished with his boat. I don't remember seeing him after that. Now if you'll excuse me, I have a lot to do at the marina. The storm surge flooded everything."

The Aldens thanked Mr. Valencia, and he hurried off.

"Eric Pruett made a big mistake yesterday," Henry said. "I wonder why."

"Maybe he didn't think the storm would be so bad," said Jessie. "Ms. Freeman didn't seem too worried yesterday."

"I still think he's hiding treasure," said Benny. "He doesn't look like a pirate, but maybe he is!"

"What about the bear?" Violet asked. "Do you think the storm surge carried it away?"

"I'm afraid it might have," Jessie said. "Poor Ms. Freeman. We won't find her bear if it's in the ocean."

Violet gasped and pointed downhill toward the marina. "The next street down is still covered in water. Look, someone is walking through the water!"

The children hurried to get a better view. "I don't think that's a person," Jessie said.

"It's too big to be a person," Henry said. "It almost looks like..."

"A bear walking on its back legs!" said Benny.

5

Follow That Bear!

As the Aldens got closer, they saw that it was a bear, but it was not walking. It was one of the town's bear statues, bobbing along in the water.

"We should try to rescue it," said Violet. "Before it floats out to sea."

Henry studied the street. "It's too dangerous to walk in the water. It might not be deep, but it's dark and murky. You can't see the ground. Let's stay on the sidewalk, where you can see the ground."

Benny jumped onto the sidewalk, laughing as water splashed up. "Let's go!"

The bear statue floated slowly along the street. They could only see the backside, but they could tell it was not Ms. Freeman's bear. Hers wore a blue overalls. This one was wearing a red jacket.

At the end of the block, the bear statue drifted downhill to a park on the waterfront. For a moment, Benny thought they had lost it. Instead, when he got to where he could see the waterfront, he saw a whole group of bear statues in the water.

"Look at all of them!" said Violet. Some of the bears were on their sides. Others were upright. It was strange to see all of the smiling, lifelike bears bobbing up and down.

"That railing is keeping them from floating out to sea," said Henry. "Let's go see if Ms. Freeman's is there."

Suddenly, one of the shapes in the water stood up straight.

"Someone is down in the water," said Jessie.

"It's Sarah from the ice-cream shop," said Violet. "What is she doing?"

"Maybe the water washed her down here too," said Benny.

They waved and called out to her, and Sarah swung around and jumped at the sight of them.

"Are you all right?" Henry asked.

"Oh, it's you." Sarah looked around. "Where's Ms. Freeman?"

"She's waiting for you in the ice-cream shop," Henry said. "You didn't show up this morning, and the phones are out."

Sarah waded toward them. The water came up to her knees in places, but she wore rubber overalls to stay dry. "We can't open the store without power," she said. "Anyway, there's too much else to do."

"The town *is* a mess," said Jessie. "What are you doing here?"

Sarah shrugged. "I thought the ice-cream bear might be in that group, but it's not." She bit her lip for a few seconds. "I really hope it didn't wash out to sea. I don't know what to do."

"Ms. Freeman is sad about losing the bear too," Violet said. "But it will be all right. The town has survived worse storms than this one, right? Ms. Freeman told us about the real bear who came to town after the last storm, and how it helped everyone work together to rebuild."

"Yeah, right," Sarah said. "The town will be fine. I'm not worried about the town." She sighed and looked back at the floating bears. "I just really, really need to find that bear."

The children looked at each other. They were surprised that Sarah was so upset about the statue. It was a great statue, but people were more important than things.

"We'll keep trying to find the ice-cream bear," Violet said.

All the children nodded. Henry said, "The other business owners will want their bears back. We should go get them."

Sarah smiled at the children. "Maybe someone will offer a reward for the return of their bear!"

"We don't need a reward," said Jessie.

"Unless it's food!" Benny said. "Is there a pizza shop bear? Let's save that one first."

Sarah chuckled. "You can have the pizza. I'll take money. You kids better wait here where it's dry. I'll pull the bears over one at a time."

Sarah waded back to the floating bears and grabbed one by the ears and dragged it through the water. At the sidewalk, she got behind the bear. "You'll have to help me get it onto dry land."

"Violet and Benny, please stand back," said Henry. "Jessie and I can take the bear from this end."

Sarah bent over and started lifting the bear. She grunted with the effort. Henry and Jessie grabbed on where they could. They got the bear standing upright on the sidewalk. "We'll push it back out of the way," Henry said. He and Jessie shuffled the bear away from the water.

"This bear must be from a bookstore," said Jessie. The bear was holding a stack of books and had reading glasses perched on its nose. "Or maybe a library."

Sarah came back with another bear statue. They got that one onto land.

"That bear has flowers," said Violet. "It could be from a flower shop."

"The bears are holding clues," said Benny. "We can use them to figure out where the statues belong."

Next Sarah brought the bear they had followed down the street. "I don't know what this one is," said Violet. "It's wearing a red jacket. Its white curly hair looks like a wig."

Follow That Bear!

"That's like a judge's wig from long ago," Jessie said. "The jacket is old-fashioned too. Maybe it's from a museum or the courthouse."

Sarah simply shrugged and headed back into the water.

Jessie whispered, "Do you think it's strange that Sarah is working so hard to get the bears out of the water? Yesterday at the shop she could hardly be bothered to scoop our ice cream."

Henry nodded. "I know what you mean," he said. "Maybe the storm gave her a change of heart."

The Aldens lined up the bears on the sidewalk. Soon Sarah brought the last one to where they were standing. It was the statue for the marina. The bear was holding a fishing pole with a big fish on the end.

Sarah used one hand to push loose hair out of her face. As she did, the bear slipped away from her other hand. The current of the water pulled it toward the ocean.

She grabbed at the bear. But it seemed to jump away from her hands. She wobbled and stumbled backward. In a few seconds, the bear would float out of reach.

Henry stepped into the water to help, but after a few steps, his foot slipped. He waved his arms, trying to find his balance. Then he fell into the murky water.

"Henry!" Violet yelled.

Benny ran forward.

"Stay back!" called Jessie. She carefully knelt at the edge of the water. "It's so dark, I can't see him. Maybe if I reach in—"

Just then, Henry's head popped up. He coughed and wiped water from his face. He smiled at his worried siblings. "I'm all right. I see why they say not to wade in floodwater after a storm. I tripped on something big under the surface."

"You scared us," Jessie said. "Come out."

"Just a minute," said Henry. "I'll help Sarah with this last bear. I'm already wet, and I have a good place to stand now."

Sarah caught up with the bear before it got back to the railing. She pushed it to the sidewalk where Henry helped lift it out. They scrambled from the water and hauled it to dry land.

"Now what do we do with them?" Violet asked.

Sarah shrugged. "I have to go. Let me know if you get a reward."

Before the Aldens could thank her, Sarah sloshed to the corner and started up the hill.

"Henry needs dry clothes," said Jessie. "Let's get Grandfather and Ms. Freeman. They will know what to do next."

Back at the ice-cream shop, they explained what had happened. Ms. Freeman said she'd take the bears to her house, where they would be safe and out of the way. That evening, she drove her truck to the waiting statues. The Aldens loaded up the bears, with the help of some other people who passed by.

The children unloaded the bears in Ms. Freeman's yard. Henry changed into dry clothes. After a hearty dinner, they cleaned up some of the fallen branches outside.

Before going to bed, the children met in the room Henry and Benny shared. "We found a lot of bears today," said Violet. "But we didn't find Ms. Freeman's bear."

"We don't know who damaged her generator

either," Henry said. "Or if it has something to do with the missing bear."

"We have a lot of mysteries," Benny said happily. "The bears, the generator, and the man with the boat in the street."

"I'm not sure that's a mystery," Jessie said.

"I'm sure I saw someone in his boat!" said Benny. "That's mysterious."

"We'll learn more tomorrow," said Henry. "We'll find out where all these bears belong. Maybe we'll find some more clues to our mysteries." He yawned.

Jessie and Violet went to their room. Henry fell asleep quickly, but Benny was too excited to sleep. When he finally did drift off, he had strange dreams about bears sailing boats.

Then something woke him from his happy dream.

Light flashed through the window. A noise came from outside. Was it another storm?

Benny hopped out of bed and pressed his face against the window. A small light bobbed through the yard. A flashlight! The light paused by a large, dark shape, one of the bear statues. Benny heard a knocking sound. Then the light moved to another statue. The knocking came again. Benny couldn't tell anything about the shadow moving among the statues.

The light moved sideways. Suddenly, it flew several feet through the air and dropped to the ground. Then Benny saw the shape of one of the big, dark statues tipping over.

Crash!

The light went out. In the moonlight, Benny saw the shadow of a person scrambling away.

Benny glanced toward Henry. Surely that crash woke him. But Henry simply rolled over and kept sleeping. They had the only bedroom on this side of the house. No one else could have heard or seen what Benny heard and saw. The person was gone, so it wouldn't help to wake everyone now.

Benny got back into bed. He lay awake, wondering: Why was someone knocking on the bear statues?

CHAPTER 6

Copies and Clues

As soon as it was light out, Benny woke Henry. Then he roused Jessie and Violet. "We need to go outside," he said.

The children got dressed and followed Benny into the yard. "Why are we out here so early?" Henry asked. "You haven't even had breakfast yet!"

"My stomach wants breakfast," said Benny, "but this is important." He told them about the shadowy person with the flashlight knocking on the bears.

"Why would someone do that?" asked Violet.

"Maybe they were looking for something," said Jessie.

Henry rapped on one of the bear statues, then on another. "They sound the same to me."

"Here's the broken one," said Jessie. The bear holding the bouquet of flowers lay on its side. The children hauled it upright.

"Oh no!" said Violet. "Its arm broke off. How sad."

Jessie picked up the broken arm. "It's a hollow shell," she said. "It could be that someone is hiding something in one of these bears."

Benny jumped up and down. "That's what the person with the flashlight wanted! They knew something was hidden in a bear."

Jessie looked at all of the statues. "Do you think they found it?"

"The person ran away when this bear fell over, right?" Henry asked Benny. "You're sure they didn't look inside this broken bear?"

"No, they ran away as soon as it fell," said Benny. "Their light went out."

The Aldens looked at the ground where the statue had fallen. There was a broken flashlight pressed into the grass.

Henry picked it up and read the words on the side. "Port Elizabeth Marina."

Copies and Clues

"Do you think Mr. Valencia was here looking for the statue for his marina?" asked Jessie.

"It's possible," said Henry. "Whoever it was didn't find what they were looking for. We need to figure out what they're searching for and find it before they do."

"Yay, another mystery!" Benny turned back to the house. "Let's figure it out after breakfast."

In the kitchen, Jessie checked the ice tray. "The ice cubes are melting. The penny is halfway down."

"That's okay," Ms. Freeman said. "Things are starting to thaw, but they won't be too warm yet."

Jessie quickly passed out the ingredients Ms. Freeman asked for.

"See, this food is fine," said Ms. Freeman. "It's the walk-in freezer at the ice-cream shop that worries me. It should be all right for now, but if I lose it...Well, I did some accounting yesterday, and I don't know if I'll be able to recover."

For the first time, it seemed like Ms. Freeman was worried about what might happen.

"It will be all right," Violet said. "The people of Port Elizabeth will get through this. They will help each other, like they helped the bear after the last big storm. The town survives."

Ms. Freeman smiled. "Thanks for the reminder," she said. "We are resilient. You can push us down, but we spring back up! And who could stay down with such a happy collection of bears in their front yard."

Ms. Freeman finished cooking breakfast and served it.

As they ate, Henry said, "We need to tell people we have the bears. But how? We can't send emails. We can't put a notice on a community website, and many people won't have working phones yet."

"We could make posters to tell where they are," Violet said. "I could draw a picture of the bears."

"We don't have a printer to make copies," said Jessie. "It will take a long time to draw each poster by hand. Then we have to post them all around town. That will take all day."

Ms. Freeman grinned. "I know a shortcut. Finish your breakfast, and I'll show you."

The children quickly ate, then they washed the dishes. Ms. Freeman led them to a cluttered workroom. She stopped in front of a machine sitting on a table. It was larger than a computer printer.

"This is a mimeograph machine," Ms. Freeman said. "It makes copies. People used these before they had photocopiers or computers with printers."

Benny leaned close, his eyes wide. "It must be really old!"

Ms. Freeman chuckled. "It's probably older than your grandfather. But mimeograph machines are still used in some places. They don't need electricity. That's handy where people don't always have power."

"How does it work?" Violet asked.

"First, you make the paper you want to copy," said Ms. Freeman. "You can use a typewriter for the text."

She showed them an old-fashioned typewriter. "This is old enough that it doesn't use electricity either. Use this special sheet of paper. It's covered with wax. Type like you would on a computer keyboard, but be careful because you can't erase mistakes."

The children talked about what they wanted

to say on the flyer. They figured out all the words before they started. Then Jessie sat at the typewriter. She fed the special paper into the top. When she pressed the keys, tiny metal hammers moved. Each little hammer stamped a letter onto the waxy paper.

After typing her message, Jessie pulled the paper out of the typewriter. "That was fun. I only had one size of letter though. I couldn't make a big headline."

"I'll draw a bear on the paper," said Violet. "People will see that and know what the flyer is about." Violet planned what she wanted. She had to scratch her drawing into the wax on the paper. She couldn't use any colors. She made a simple outline of a bear holding a stack of books.

Ms. Freeman took the flyer. "Now we put this stencil in the mimeograph machine. We wrap it tightly around this cylinder." She did that. "Now someone adds the ink."

Henry found the bottle of ink. He poured it into the machine's roller. "Oops. I got some on my thumb," he said. "My thumb is purple from the ink!"

Grandfather chuckled. "We say that someone who is good with plants has a green thumb. I don't know what having a purple thumb means."

"I guess it means I'm fond of Violet," Henry said, giving his sister a playful nudge.

Benny leaned close to the machine. "Can I help?"

"Of course," said Ms. Freeman. "You can run the hand crank. This handle turns the cylinder. It presses against the roller filled with ink. The ink gets into the stencil made in the wax. Then the ink is transferred onto paper." She put a stack of paper into the machine.

Benny turned the crank. Around and around it went! The machine spit out page after page. Each one had the flyer printed on it. "I think this is faster than our printer at home!" Benny said. Soon they had thirty copies.

"Now people will know where to find their bears," Jessie said.

"This might be the best thing you can do for Port Elizabeth," Grandfather said. "Having the bears back in place will boost people's spirits."

Violet studied a flyer. "Maybe someone knows

where the ice-cream bear is. If they see this, they
might let us know."

Grandfather drove them through town, and the
children put up the flyers.

"The rest of the flyers can go on Main Street
and the marina," said Grandfather. "I'll park at the

ice-cream shop and you can walk."

He stopped outside the shop, and the Aldens went in to see if Ms. Freeman needed help.

Sarah was behind the counter with her back to the door. "Hi, Sarah," said Jessie. "It looks like things are starting to get back to normal around here."

"I know you were supposed to have the necklace today," Sarah said, and at first Jessie thought Sarah was talking to her. Then she saw Sarah was talking on the shop's landline telephone. "I'll get it to you as soon as I can. Everything is a mess here. I need to go." Sarah hung up with a big sigh.

"Can we help with anything?" Violet asked.

Sarah turned to them. She shook her head. "No, no, it's fine. Just one of my jewelry customers. She doesn't understand how the storm messed everything up."

"Did you lose some of your jewelry?" Jessie asked.

Sarah mumbled something. Then she quickly said, "Hey, are you still searching for our bear? Have you found it?"

"Not yet," Violet said.

Benny rose up on his toes to look over the counter. "We're finding clues! Last night someone came to the yard and looked at all the bears. Did you know they're hollow inside? We think something is hidden in a bear."

"Really?" Sarah shrugged and looked away. "That's odd. It doesn't seem very likely. Why would anyone do that? I'm sure you're mistaken." She came out from behind the counter, still talking. "Sorry I can't serve you any ice cream today. Marie won't open the deep freeze until we have power again. I only came in to use the phone. Well, bye!" The door swung closed behind Sarah before anyone could say anything more.

"That was strange," said Jessie.

A moment later, Ms. Freeman came in from the back room. "Did Sarah just leave?" she asked.

The children nodded. "She mentioned something about her online jewelry store."

"Oh, of course. The Ice Box—that's the name of her shop. Having the Internet down must be hard for her. Still, she has been acting very strangely lately."

"This storm has been hard on lots of people,"

Violet said. "We should post the rest of the flyers. Once the bears are back in place, people will feel better."

Grandfather stayed in the shop to help Ms. Freeman, and the children went to post the flyers.

Outside, George Williams stood in front of The Stylish Sailor, frowning at another man.

"I delivered," the second man insisted. "I did exactly what I was told."

Benny stared for a second. He turned to the others and whispered, "That's the guy whose boat was in the street!"

Henry nodded. It was Eric Pruett, and he did not seem happy. Henry pulled the others back into the doorway of the ice-cream shop. He did not want to eavesdrop, but even through the glass, they could hear George Williams's speak with his southern accent.

"I told ya," said Mr. Williams. "I don't know what you're talkin' about. Stop pestering me, please." He turned and went into his shop.

"But I need my money!" Mr. Pruett said. He stared after Mr. Williams for a minute. Then he ducked his head and hurried away.

Jessie said, "Eric Pruett thinks George Williams owes him money. Mr. Williams says no. Which of them is right?"

Benny grinned. "It's another mystery!"

Getting Warmer, Getting Cooler

The Alden children walked down Main Street looking for places to put up flyers. The bookstore owner was delighted to hear that they had found her bear. She put a flyer in the store window. The flower shop was closed. Jessie wrote a note on the back of a flyer about that bear's broken arm. She tucked the flyer under the door handle.

When they finished on Main Street, the children headed for the marina. "The water has gone down a lot," Jessie said. "It's almost back to normal."

"Look!" Benny said. "That's the boat that was in the street yesterday."

The Aldens walked toward the red and white boat. It sat atop a trailer near the water. Henry said, "Mr. Pruett must have found a way to move his boat."

The Aldens circled the boat and trailer for a closer look. "Oh, hello," said Jessie as they came across Hector Valencia.

The marina manager was frowning at the boat. "Hi, kids," he said. "Do you see anything wrong with this vessel?"

They studied the large boat. "The side is scraped," said Henry. "That window is cracked. But it doesn't look too badly damaged."

"It looks good for a boat that sailed onto land," Jessie said.

Mr. Valencia nodded. "The damage is mainly on the surface. I don't see any cracks or holes in the hull." He patted the side of the boat. "This boat could go back in the water right now."

"I'd like to see that!" said Benny.

"So would I," Mr. Valencia said. "But Eric won't do it. He didn't take the boat out of the water. Now he doesn't want it put back in! He says he needs to fix it first. But is he fixing it? No, he is not. It's sitting here in the way. As long as it floats, he could leave it in the water until he's ready to work on it."

"Can't you move it?" asked Jessie.

"I could," Mr. Valencia said. "But Eric Pruett is always short on money. I'm afraid he'd blame me for the boat's damage and want me to pay." He shook his head. "No, I have to wait for Eric to take action. Anyway, the inspectors are busy."

"The ones who were looking for smugglers?" asked Henry.

"Have they found any pirates yet?" Benny asked.

Mr. Valencia chuckled. "Smugglers don't attack other ships, like pirates do. Smugglers carry illegal goods. We can't put the boat back in the water until Eric has had it inspected."

"Does that take long?" Jessie asked.

"Not on a boat this size. Eric simply needs to schedule the inspection." Mr. Valencia looked at the boat and sighed. "Most people who keep boats are great. They take care of themselves and each other. But I have to put up with a lot from Eric. I think he's awake more at night than in the day. He takes his boat in and out at strange hours. His engine is loud, so it wakes people sleeping on other

boats. I get complaints."

That reminded Jessie of something. She pulled out the broken flashlight they had found in Ms. Freeman's grass. "Do you recognize this?" she asked.

Mr. Valencia took the flashlight and looked it over. "Of course," he said. "We give these away here at the marina. It looks like this one has seen better days. Where did you find it?"

Jessie told Mr. Valencia about the statues they had collected, including the marina's fishing bear. She also told him about the nighttime visitor who had been snooping around Ms. Freeman's house.

"I'm glad to hear you found the marina's bear," said Mr. Valencia. "We've been missing her around here. I'm afraid I can't help you with the flashlight though. Many people have those. We give them to everyone who rents space at the marina."

The Aldens thanked Mr. Valencia for his time and went on to post the rest of their flyers.

As they walked, Jessie said, "Mr. Pruett sure is acting strange. First, he was arguing with Mr. Williams. Then he wouldn't move his boat...It seems like he's up to something."

"Do you think he was the person who dropped the flashlight?" asked Benny.

The children thought about this for a moment. Henry said, "He probably has a flashlight because he has a spot at the marina, but a lot of people have those flashlights. Why he would care about the bears?"

Jessie nodded. "There's something special about those statues," she said. "We just need to figure out what it is."

When the children got back to the shop, Grandfather was waiting outside. Ms. Freeman had closed down for the day and gone home.

Back at the house, she greeted them with a big smile. "Your flyers are working already!" she said. "People have been coming to pick up their bears. The statues aren't too heavy, but they are awkward. You need three or four people and a truck to move one of those statues. Everyone is working together. They've been talking and laughing. They're sharing their problems and helping out."

Violet clasped her hands together. "How wonderful!"

Getting Warmer, Getting Cooler

Ms. Freeman nodded. "It feels like we are one big family. In fact, I talked to Gloria Chang at the fish market. I told her about the generator problem. She's going to let me use her freezer space for my ice cream."

"That's great news, Marie," said Grandfather.

Benny went to the window and looked out on the yard where they'd put the statues. "You have a few bears left. Is that Sarah out there with them?"

"Yes, she arrived a little while ago," said Ms. Freeman. "I told her about what happened last night, and she wanted to see the bear with the broken arm."

"It looks like she's interested in all the bears," said Benny. Sarah was walking around the yard, examining each one closely.

"She's an artist," Violet noted. "Maybe she thinks she can help clean up and fix the bears."

Jessie went to the window as well. "There's the fishing bear. Mr. Valencia should be picking that one up soon."

"The flower shop bear has a date tonight too," said Ms. Freeman. "The store owners are borrowing a truck. They thought they could be here about eight." She looked at her watch. "Let's have an early dinner. I need to get to my shop and take the ice cream over to Gloria at the fish market. Sarah offered to stay here. She'll watch the bears and greet people who come for them."

"Don't you want her help moving the ice cream?" Grandfather asked.

"She said she hurt her back moving those bears out of the water," Ms. Freeman said. "I don't want her to strain it more."

"We'll all help with the ice cream," said Henry.

Jessie checked the freezer. "The ice cubes are melted almost all the way. These frozen foods won't last much longer without power."

They cleaned out the freezer, and Ms. Freeman cooked everything. They had an interesting dinner. They could choose from hamburgers, baked chicken, french fries, egg rolls, fish sticks, and mixed vegetables. Benny had a little bit of everything.

Sarah joined them for dinner. She seemed distracted and kept getting up to look out the window at the bears. As soon as she finished eating, she went outside again.

As the Aldens finished dinner, Mr. Valencia drove up with an assistant.

"We'll clean up," Henry told Ms. Freeman.

Ms. Freeman and Grandfather went outside to help with the fishing bear.

The children carried the dishes to the sink and started washing them. "Let's think about our mysteries," said Henry.

Jessie pulled out her notebook. "I'll make notes," she said. "What do we know?"

The Aldens wrote down what they had talked about at the marina about the boat owner, Eric Pruett.

"Mr. Pruett is acting strangely," said Jessie. "But that is not a crime. We are looking for the person who broke the generator at the ice-cream shop. Why would he do that?"

"Maybe he is working with George Williams," said Violet. "We saw them arguing about money outside the shop. Maybe George hired Eric to hurt the ice-cream shop."

"Maybe," said Violet. "But Mr. Williams didn't seem like he knew what Eric was talking about."

"Perhaps George hired Mr. Pruett, but then he didn't want to pay him after all," Jessie suggested.

"That would be risky," said Henry. "If he doesn't get paid, Mr. Pruett might tell everyone about their deal."

Benny went to the window and looked out. "Sarah is acting funny too. She's really worried about all the bears."

"She does seem very interested in finding the ice-cream bear," Jessie said. "I understand why Ms. Freeman wants it back. It's her shop and her bear. But Sarah doesn't act worried about Ms. Freeman. It's like she wants the bear for her own reasons."

Henry dried the last of the dishes and hung up the towel. "Remember the night the power went out?" he asked. "Sarah was the last person to leave the ice-cream shop."

"Maybe she turned off the generator!" Violet said. "Wait, someone broke the lock to get to the generator. Would Sarah have a key?"

"Maybe not," said Henry. "An employee would

not usually need to get to the generator."

"I know who would have a key," Jessie said. "George Williams. Ms. Freeman said the generator was for her shop and his. He wouldn't need to break the lock to get to in."

"Good point," said Henry.

Benny turned from the window. "Maybe he broke the lock to make it look like he didn't have a key."

Violet flopped into a chair. "We have too many suspects and too many clues. We need new information. The trail is growing cold."

"And the ice cream is getting warm," Benny said.

Henry laughed. "We are going to make the ice cream cold again. Maybe then we'll get a hot trail."

CHAPTER 8

The Bear Trap

The Aldens went into town with Ms. Freeman to bring the ice cream to the fish market. As they drove up to the ice-cream shop, Benny shouted, "Look, look!"

The others peered out the windows of Ms. Freeman's pickup truck. "Why, we have a visitor!" said Jessie.

Standing outside the shop, right where it belonged, was the ice-cream bear. After Ms. Freeman pulled up, Benny ran out and gave the bear a hug. Violet patted its arm. Henry looked it over. "It needs a wash, but otherwise it looks fine," he said.

"How on earth did it get here?" Ms. Freeman asked.

The Bear Trap

The door to The Stylish Sailor opened, and Mr. Williams stepped out. "Your bear came a-wanderin' back," he said.

"Do you know how it got here?" Ms. Freeman asked.

Mr. Williams nodded. "Some folks who live out on a houseboat found it down by the waterfront. I guess it was in the same park where you kids found all those other bears."

"That's strange," said Jessie. "We rescued every bear statue there. I'm sure we didn't miss any."

"From what I heard, most of those statues floated, correct?" asked Mr. Williams.

"That's right," said Henry. "They're hollow."

"Well, apparently this one didn't float," said Mr. Williams. "It lay facedown on the ground. It was hidden until the water level dropped."

Henry gasped. "I bet I tripped on this bear when I fell in the water," he said. "I was right on top of it and didn't know!"

"I'm so glad it's back home again," Ms. Freeman said. "It makes me believe everything will be all right. Now, I need to talk to Gloria. I want to make sure her freezer has space ready. Then we can move the ice cream from my big freezer."

"Do you kids want to come with us or wait here?" Grandfather asked.

"We'll wait here," said Henry. "We can clean up the bear."

Ms. Freeman unlocked the ice-cream shop. "You'll find cleaning supplies in the closet," she said. "Thank you for doing that."

Mr. Williams went back into his store. Grandfather and Ms. Freeman headed down the street. The children clustered around the ice-cream bear.

"I want to check this statue," Henry said. "Why didn't it float when the others did?"

Jessie knocked on the bear's shoulder. "It sounds like the others."

Henry rocked the bear from side to side. "Do you hear that sloshing sound? I think some water got inside."

"We can clean it and take a good, close look," said Jessie.

The Aldens got spray cleaner and towels from the closet. They filled a bucket with water and started scrubbing. Henry examined the bear's head as he washed it. He pulled on the ears and pressed the eyes and nose. "Nothing strange here," he said.

Jessie polished the bear's back. "Everything looks normal here," she said.

Violet carefully washed the ice-cream cone. "Look at this," she said. "A line goes around the top of the cone, right above the bear's hands. I think the ice cream is a separate piece."

Benny jumped up and down. "Pull on it! Maybe you found a secret opening."

Violet pulled on the cone, but nothing happened. She tried to turn the stack of ice cream to the left. It didn't budge. She turned it to the right. "It's moving!" she said. She twisted the ice-cream scoops halfway around. They popped right off.

The children peered into the small opening in the bear's hands. "Some water must have gotten in through the crack," said Henry. "That helped weigh it down, so it didn't float."

Jessie looked closer. "I think I see something," she said. She reached her arm into the statue and pulled out a small cloth bag.

"Yuck, it's all wet and dirty," Violet said.

Benny leaned in to get a better look. "What do you think is inside?" he asked.

"There's only one way to find out." Jessie pulled open the drawstring and tipped the bag to pour out its contents.

Dozens of jewels spilled into her hand.

The children gasped. Violet picked up a jewel that had fallen onto the ground. She held up the red stone so the light shined through it. "I don't think these are plastic or glass. They look real!"

Henry looked up and down the street. A dozen people were walking or cleaning up their stores. Something moved in the boutique next door. Was Mr. Williams looking out the window?

"Let's take these inside," Henry said. "Who knows who is watching."

The children put the ice-cream scoops back onto the statue and went into the shop. Henry made sure the Closed sign showed on the door.

The Aldens sat around the table and studied the jewels. "We wanted another clue," said Jessie. "I guess we found one."

"What does it mean?" Violet asked.

"Pirates!" said Benny.

Henry grinned. "You're not too far off. Mr. Valencia told us about smugglers. Remember? That's why they are inspecting all the boats. This must be what they're searching for."

"I get it," said Jessie. "Someone is bringing the jewels on a boat to Port Elizabeth. Then they're sneaking them ashore so they don't have to pay the taxes. They hide the jewels in the bear, then someone else comes and picks them up."

"Why are they using the happy bear?" Violet asked. "I can't believe Ms. Freeman knows about this."

"I don't think she does," said Henry. "She wouldn't leave us alone to wash the bear if she knew it was hiding jewels."

"Who is it then?" asked Benny.

The children thought for a moment. Then Henry snapped his fingers and stood up. He went to the window and looked out.

"Remember what Ms. Freeman said about the generator?" he asked. "When the power goes down, it keeps the ice cream cold *and* it keeps the security system going. There's a camera that looks over the front of the store. Without power, the security camera wouldn't work."

"That's why the person broke the generator!" said Jessie. "It wasn't to melt the ice cream. It was to turn off the security camera! They didn't want the camera to record them putting the jewels in the secret hiding place."

Violet gathered the jewels back into the bag. "I'll hide these in the closet. We can find the inspectors tomorrow and give them the jewels. But they still won't know who the smugglers are. We haven't caught the person yet."

"The smugglers must be desperate to find it," said Jessie. "Whoever wants these jewels will check the bear soon. Maybe we can catch them in the act."

"But how?" asked Violet. "They will probably come at night. We can't stay here and watch for them."

"And the security cameras still don't work," Henry said. "We'll have to find another way to catch the smuggler."

"We have done a lot without electricity," said Benny. "We made phone calls and listened to the radio. Jessie typed the flyer with a typewriter. We printed it with that old machine. And we ate lots of food before it went bad!"

Henry smiled. "I see what you're saying, Benny. We can do it the old-fashioned way. We just need a way to identify the person. But how?" Henry tapped his fingers on the table as he thought.

"Henry, your thumb!" said Violet. "It's still purple."

"Yes, it's from the ink we used for the flyers," said Henry. "It's impossible to wash out."

Violet explained. If they could mark the smuggler with ink during the night, the children would then be able to find the person during the day. All they needed to do was put ink inside the hidden compartment. When the person reached in, the ink would stain their hands.

"Great idea, Violet," Henry said. "Now, how will we know if someone has opened the bear? We can't keep opening it to check the ink. Someone might notice."

Jessie had an idea. "Remember the penny in the ice tray?" she said. "When the ice melted, the penny sank. If the ice froze again, you could still tell what had happened. Maybe we can do something like that."

Benny did not understand. He scrunched up his face and asked, "You want to put ice and pennies in the statue?"

Jessie laughed. "No. I want to set a trap to find out if someone looked inside the bear. It doesn't have to use ice cubes or pennies. It only has to show us that something has changed."

Henry tried to explain. "Remember that detective story Grandfather read us?" he asked. "The detective taped a strand of hair across the crack in the doorframe. When somebody went through the door, the hair broke. That was how the detective found out someone had been inside."

"Oh, I get it," said Violet. "The hair in the door lets us know the door has been opened and closed again, just like the penny in the ice cube lets us know the ice has melted and frozen again."

"That's right!" said Jessie. "But I don't think we need to use a hair."

Jessie went into the shop and came out with two pieces of clear tape and a thin piece of napkin. She held the napkin up to the cone. The color matched almost perfectly.

"It blends right in," said Jessie. "The thief won't even see it! They will open up the bear, and the napkin will rip."

"But we *will* see it because we know what to look for," said Violet. "If the napkin is ripped in the morning, we will know someone came looking for the jewels."

Benny jumped up. "Then we'll catch the thief purple-handed!"

CHAPTER 9

Treasure on a Trailer

Ms. Freeman's house was only a mile away, so Henry ran back there. Sarah was in the side yard when he arrived, helping with the flower shop bear. Henry snuck inside the house and got the ink container from the mimeograph machine. Then the children spent the evening setting up their trap and moving ice cream.

In the morning, they could hardly wait to get to the shop. Ms. Freeman walked up to the door. "Sarah isn't here yet," she said. "I guess the storm really threw off her schedule. I hope it's nothing more serious, but still, I did ask her to come in today."

Grandfather and Ms. Freeman went inside. The

children hurried over to the ice-cream bear.

"Look," whispered Violet, pointing at the ground. On the sidewalk, a trail of purple dots led away from the bear.

Henry looked closely at the napkin. It was ripped right across the middle. "Someone definitely fell for our trap."

Benny jumped up and down. "We did the trick! We did the trick!" he said.

"That's right," said Jessie. "Now we just need to figure out who was here."

The children went into the ice-cream shop. "Marie is out back with the repairman," Grandfather said. "Hopefully, he can get the generator going soon. There's not much for you to do here at the moment."

"That's okay," said Henry. "We'll take a walk through town."

As the children left the shop, Benny said, "We're going to look for the thief, right?"

Henry nodded. "Maybe we can find some of our suspects. We'll see if they have purple spots on their hands."

Jessie pointed to the shop next door. "I don't think Mr. Williams is our smuggler. But he is still a suspect."

The Aldens studied the fancy shop for a moment. They knew Mr. Williams did not like children in the store. Finally, Violet said, "Henry, you are the oldest. You had better go in alone."

Jessie, Violet, and Benny waited outside while Henry went into the boutique. He joined them a few minutes later.

"Was he mean?" Violet asked.

"No," said Henry. "I said we might want to buy a present for Mrs. McGregor. I asked about the scarves in the window."

"Oh, we should get her one!" Violet said. "They're pretty."

Henry nodded. "Mr. Williams was friendly. He joked that I was welcome as long as I didn't have ice cream. I didn't see any ink on his hands when he was showing me the scarves."

"Who's our next suspect?" Violet asked.

"How about Eric Pruett?" said Jessie. "We think the smuggler uses a boat. And we know his boat has not been inspected yet."

"And he was demanding money from Mr. Williams," added Henry.

"And I saw a ghost in his boat!" said Benny.

Jessie laughed. "Now *that* would be a twist," she said, "a ghost with purple hands."

The children walked to the marina. Mr. Pruett's boat still sat on its trailer. The children stopped to study the boat. "Someone is moving inside," Jessie said. She bit her lip. "I'm getting nervous. Maybe we shouldn't confront him without an adult."

"I see Mr. Valencia out on the dock," said Violet. "If anyone is smuggling jewels here, he will want to know about it."

They asked Mr. Valencia if he would come with them to talk to Mr. Pruett.

The marina manager agreed. "I need to find out his plans anyway," he said. "I left him a message yesterday and asked him to come see me as soon as possible. I didn't realize he was here now."

The group approached the boat. "How do we let him know we're here?" Violet asked. "Should we knock on the side of the boat?"

Mr. Valencia frowned and shook his head. "Usually you ask for permission to come aboard. That's polite among people with boats. But Eric has been avoiding me, and I must talk to him. We'll go in."

They climbed a ladder set against the side of the boat. Mr. Valencia led the way to the cabin door. He knocked and pushed open the door. "Eric!"

Mr. Pruett hurried toward them. "What's going on? You can't come in here!"

Mr. Valencia pushed through the door. "You're on marina property. If you're hiding something, it's my right to know."

The children gathered behind him. They looked around the cabin, which was still damp from the storm.

"Look!" Benny said. "It's the bald person with red earrings!"

Benny pointed to a piece of foam in the shape of a head and shoulders. Around the neck was a fancy-looking piece of jewelry.

"A mannequin head!" said Violet. "That is what you must have seen in the window, Benny."

Jessie crossed the cabin. Several piles of colorful stones lay on a small table. "Look at these jewels!" she said. "They look like the ones hidden in the bear statue."

Mr. Pruett dropped into a chair. He rubbed his face with his hands and groaned.

"What's all this?" Mr. Valencia asked. "A bear statue with jewels? You'd better explain."

The children took turns explaining what they knew. They told Mr. Valencia about the missing ice-cream bear. They described its return and how they found the jewels.

"You said the inspectors were looking for smugglers," Henry said. "We thought someone might be bringing the jewels in on a boat and putting them in the bear for someone else to pick up."

"We set a trap!" Benny blurted. He told Mr. Valencia how they'd put ink in the bear's hidden compartment.

"That was very clever," said Mr. Valencia. "Eric, would you please hold out your hands?"

Mr. Pruett held out his hands. They were clean.

Mr. Valencia frowned, but Henry explained.

"That means he did not try to get the jewels *out* of the bear. He might have put them *in* the bear before the storm."

"Eric, do you have anything to say?" asked Mr. Valencia.

Mr. Pruett sighed. "The children are right. Maybe it's for the best. I've been sick with worry the last few days."

"Is that because you thought the storm had washed away the bear, along with the jewels you put there?" asked Jessie.

Eric Pruett nodded. "I brought the jewels in on my boat. I bought them in Central America. I did not steal them! But I didn't declare the jewels when I brought them into the country. I didn't pay the taxes."

"That's why you didn't leave the harbor before the storm," said Henry. "You didn't want to have your boat inspected."

"You took a big risk," said Mr. Valencia. "You're lucky your boat wasn't destroyed or lost at sea."

"I know," said Mr. Pruett. "That storm scared the pants off me. When my boat washed up and that bear went missing, I thought I'd lose everything. I wanted to make a little extra money, not lose it."

"You came to Ms. Freeman's in the middle of the night, didn't you?" said Benny. "You were looking for the ice-cream bear!"

Mr. Pruett nodded glumly.

"We heard you ask George Williams for money," said Henry. "Was he the person you were delivering the jewels to?"

"I never knew who picked up the jewels," said Mr. Pruett. "I just left them in the bear. The buyer would leave the money in the same place the next night. I thought Mr. Williams might be the buyer. He has that fancy shop."

"We don't think Mr. Williams is part of this," said Henry.

Mr. Pruett shrugged. "All I know is the person's code name. That's another reason I thought it might be Williams. He's from Georgia."

"What is the code name?" Jessie asked.

"The buyer goes by Savannah," Mr. Pruett said. "That's a city in Georgia."

The children looked at one another. Savannah

was also the name of a person. A person who had been acting very strangely.

Benny grinned and said, "Did we just solve the mystery?"

Cleaning Up Clues

"We need to talk to Savannah," said Jessie. "She might be at the ice-cream shop now."

Mr. Valencia nodded. He turned to Mr. Pruett. "The inspectors need to know about this. Do you want to tell them, or should I?"

Mr. Pruett stood up. "I'll do it."

"That will be better for you," Mr. Valencia said. "You'll have to pay the import taxes and a fine. If you cooperate, you might stay out of jail."

"That's the best I can hope for now," Mr. Pruett said. "I'm glad all this is over. Trying to get easy money was the hardest thing I've ever done!"

The two men went to find the inspectors. The children headed back to the ice-cream shop. Sarah was behind the counter. She wore yellow rubber gloves that came up to her elbows. Grandfather and Ms. Freeman sat at a table with a stack of paper between them.

"Good news," Grandfather said. "The generator isn't broken."

"That's right," Ms. Freeman said. "The vandal just removed a piece. The mechanic has replaced it. He's doing a tune-up. We should have power soon."

"Hooray!" said Benny. "Then we can bring the ice cream back. We'll have to sample each flavor to make sure it's still good though."

"We have another job to do first," Henry said. "We need to talk to Sarah—or should I say 'Savannah'?"

Sarah glanced at the children. "Since we can't open yet, I'm cleaning the food-prep area," she said, turning away and scrubbing the sink.

"This is important," said Jessie. "Can you stop a minute?"

Sarah frowned like she might want to argue. Finally, she put down her sponge and slowly came around the counter. Her rubber gloves were still on.

Cleaning Up Clues

"I like your necklace," said Violet. "Are you wearing any of your homemade bracelets today?"

Sarah shook her head. "Not while I clean."

"Can we see your hands?" asked Henry.

Sarah took a step backward. "I told you I'm not wearing any bracelets. There's nothing to see."

"What's this all about?" Ms. Freeman asked.

Sarah pulled out a chair and sat with a deep sigh. "The children know. You set up that trap, didn't you?" She slowly peeled off her gloves. Purple marks dotted both of her hands.

"You are the other smuggler!" Benny said.

Ms. Freeman gasped. "What?"

"It's true," Sarah said. "I'm so sorry."

"We saw piles of jewels in Eric Pruett's ship," said Henry. "He went to talk to the inspectors."

"Why don't you tell us your part of the story?" Violet said kindly.

"It all started after the big storm two years ago," Sarah said. "My cottage was badly damaged. The storm tore off part of the roof. Water got inside. I had to tear out the carpets. It took months to fix the roof."

Cleaning Up Clues

"I didn't know the storm hit you so bad," said Ms. Freeman.

"Lots of people had it worse," Sarah said. "Everyone was busy. Everyone had bad things happen. I didn't want to ask for help or money, so I needed to make more money. I set up my online jewelry business, The Ice Box. But it's hard to make much that way. If I got the stones cheaper, that would save money."

"You arranged for Eric Pruett to smuggle the jewels," Henry said.

"I heard he needed money too," said Sarah. "His boat is big enough to get to other countries to buy the stones. It's small enough for him to run it without a crew."

"He says he didn't know who got the jewels," said Jessie.

"That's right," said Sarah. "I contacted him online. I used my jewelry business name, Savannah. I was afraid to have him know who I really was. I simply told him to bring the jewels at night and put them in the bear statue. I got here early in the morning so I could collect the jewels.

I pretended I was wiping down the bear statue. Nobody noticed what I was really doing."

"What about the security camera?" Ms. Freeman asked. "I don't usually look at the recordings. I just want them in case we had a problem overnight. But you couldn't be sure I wouldn't check."

"I got a delivery every two weeks," said Sarah. "On those days, I made an excuse to stay late and turned off the shop's power before I left. That way I could be sure the security cameras wouldn't work. In the morning, I got here early and turned the power back on. If you noticed that the camera didn't record some night, you'd blame a power surge."

"That's why the ice cream was soft some mornings," Ms. Freeman said. "It got runny on nights you turned the power off."

Sarah nodded. "The power was only off for a few hours. The ice cream didn't melt enough to go bad. But on the night of the storm, I was expecting Eric Pruett to drop off jewels. I realized the storm might shut down the power to all these buildings. Then the backup generator would turn on. The security camera would go back on as soon as it had power again. I couldn't let that happen."

"You broke the generator?" Ms. Freeman asked. She sounded hurt.

"I didn't break it," Sarah said. "I took a piece off to make sure it wouldn't work. I thought I could fix it as soon as I'd picked up the jewels. Then the bear went missing. I didn't know what to do! I was afraid to put the power back on. Once the camera was working, I wouldn't be able to get the jewels."

Ms. Freeman took out a handkerchief and blew her nose. "I wish you'd told me about your money problems."

Sarah bowed her head. "I didn't want to ask for any favors. I wanted to take care of the problem myself. Instead, I made a mess of things. I'm sorry for all the trouble I caused."

"People in this town look out for one another," Ms. Freeman said. "You should have trusted us to help you." She reached over to pat Sarah's purple-stained hand.

Sarah looked up with tears in her eyes. "I made a lot of mistakes. It's time to take responsibility. I'll turn myself in and face the consequences."

Just then, the shop lights turned on. Equipment started humming.

"We have power again!" Ms. Freeman said.

"Hooray!" said Benny. "We should celebrate with ice cream. Sarah should have some before she has to talk to those inspectors."

Grandfather smiled. "Don't forget, the ice cream is over at the fish market."

Benny's nose wrinkled. Fish was one flavor that did not sound good—even to him.

The shop door opened, and Mr. Williams entered. "Hello, folks," he said. "My lights came on next door. I guess you got the generator going."

"That's right," said Ms. Freeman. "Now we can get back in business."

"About that..." Mr. Williams trailed off. He looked down at his feet.

Ms. Freeman sighed. "George, I know you don't like this place."

He shook his head. "No. No," he said. "I'd like to apologize. I should not have been so hard on you. I thought this street didn't have room for The Stylish Sailor and your ice-cream shop. That was selfish."

He smiled at the children. "Seeing how you kids helped out after the storm made me realize that. Y'all brought this town together, and you don't even live here. It made me take a hard look at what I've done since I came to town...Anyway, I wanted to apologize."

Mr. Williams offered his hand to Ms. Freeman, and she shook it.

"Do you want to help someone?" Violet asked. "Sarah makes beautiful jewelry. You could sell some in your store."

Mr. Williams looked at Sarah's earrings. "Did you make those?"

Sarah nodded. "I've been selling them online."

"They're beautiful," Mr. Williams said. "I bet I can get a lot more for them in the shop than you make online. Stop by sometime, and we'll work out a deal."

"I will." Sarah smiled. "Once I get some things straightened out."

"I also wanted to give you kids something as a thank-you," said Mr. Williams, handing a bag to Henry. "It's a scarf for your housekeeper. I hope she'll enjoy wearing it. And I hope seeing it will remind you of how you helped this town."

"So you like the bear outside now?" Jessie asked.

"Well, I may not go that far." Mr. Williams grinned. "But I am happy things are getting back to normal. Even if 'normal' means silly statues and kids with sticky hands." He waved and left the store.

Sarah stood up and said, "I should go find the inspectors."

"I'll come with you," said Ms. Freeman. "Don't worry, we'll survive this too."

Violet pulled the bag of jewels out of its hiding place. "You can take these. We weren't sure where to turn them in."

"While you do that, we can start moving the ice cream back here," said Henry.

"No rush," said Ms. Freeman. "It will take a couple of hours for the big freezer to get cold again."

"Good," said Benny. "We have something very important to do first."

Violet frowned. "Did we forget part of the

mystery? We found the ice-cream bear. We are turning in the jewels. We know who brought them to Port Elizabeth. We know who sold them. I can't think of anything we missed."

"You're forgetting the most important thing of all!" Benny said. "We haven't had *lunch*."

They all laughed. "Lunch it is," said Grandfather. "We'll move the ice cream back here this afternoon."

"Thank you all," said Ms. Freeman. "Later today, I'll give you *my* thank-you gift."

Benny bounced in his chair. "Is it ice cream?" he asked.

Ms. Freeman grinned and nodded. "It's a big bowl with a scoop of every kind of ice cream I serve," she said. "I'll bet even you won't be able to finish it."

Benny's eyes got huge. "I can't wait to try!" He grinned. "We didn't get to see the whole tall ships festival. We didn't have power for days. But this week had mysteries, helping people, and ice cream. Who needs power when you have all that?"

Turn the page to read a
sneak preview of

SECRET ON THE THIRTEENTH FLOOR

the new
Boxcar Children mystery!

It was a sunny day in early May. The trees were alive with birdsong, and the Alden children were hard at work in their front yard. Henry raked grass clippings into a large pile in the middle of the lawn. Then he tilted down a garbage can so his younger brother, Benny, could scoop them inside.

Near the front steps, Violet wore a pair of purple gardening gloves and used a spade to dig a row of evenly spaced holes in the dark soil of the garden beds. Her sister, Jessie, carried trays of flowers from their grandfather's car around to the front of the house, carefully stepping around their dog, Watch, who lay snoozing in the sun. The plastic containers held snapdragons, geraniums, and pansies.

"I just love spring," Violet said as she wiped a spot of dirt off her cheek with her forearm. She gazed at the collection of peach, red, yellow, pink, and white blossoms.

"Me too!" Jessie said. "It's the most colorful season—that's for sure."

"I love getting outside after being cooped up all winter," Henry added. As the oldest of the Alden children, at fourteen, he was getting stronger every month, and Grandfather appreciated his help with all the outdoor chores.

The Aldens hadn't always spent their days this way. After their parents died in a car accident, the four children were supposed to go live with their grandfather right away. But they had been afraid he would be mean and that they wouldn't like living with him. So instead, Henry, Jessie, Violet, and Benny had run away to the woods, where they'd found an abandoned boxcar and made it into a home. They'd discovered Watch in the woods too and had made him part of their family.

When Grandfather Alden found them, the children realized he was not mean at all! They were excited to move into the house he lived in with his housekeeper, Mrs. McGregor. Of course, Watch came along too, and Grandfather Alden set the boxcar up in his backyard for the children to use as a playhouse. Now they loved living in a neighborhood.

Back in the front yard, Benny suddenly leaped to the side and sent his armload of grass clippings fluttering back down to the lawn. He covered his face and then peeked out through his fingers at something buzzing near his head. "Bees are the only bad news about spring," he said.

"Don't bother that bee, and he won't bother you," Jessie said. She was twelve and very sensible about things that worried some children, especially Benny. "Pollinators are a very important part of the ecosystem," she added. "If we didn't have bees, we wouldn't have honey."

"Not only that," Henry added, "but seeing bees is a sign. Mrs. McGregor learned that from her aunt in Ireland. When you see bees buzzing around your house or near your windows, it means a visitor will soon arrive. And you should never try to kill the bee, because that means the visitor will bring bad news."

Benny thought this over while he stood very still, watching the black-and-yellow creature zoom past his face. He didn't like the idea of the bee

being a sign. Soon the buzzing stopped. He waited another moment to be sure the bee was gone and then used the rake to gather the fallen clippings. The work seemed to go fast when he thought about good things—like the famous honey cake Mrs. McGregor liked to make in the summer.

"Is anybody else getting hungry?" Benny asked.

Henry smiled and looked at his watch. "It *is* almost lunchtime," he said. "Maybe we should head inside and wash up."

Just as he was leaning the rake up against the front porch, a white van pulled up in front of their house.

Benny's eyes went wide, and he looked at Henry. At the same time, they both said, "A visitor!"

"Hello, children!" called Ms. Singleton, getting out of the van. Ms. Singleton was the mail carrier assigned to the Aldens' neighborhood. Like most mail carriers, she wore navy blue shorts, but on her feet were bright-pink hiking boots. She also wore a pink scarf tied inside the collar of her blue work shirt.

"You are earning your keep today, I see," Ms.

Singleton said when she saw all the work the Aldens had done on the yard.

"We don't mind," Jessie said. "Especially on such a beautiful day."

Ms. Singleton shuffled through a pile of mail she held under her arm and pulled out a catalog and two letters. "Not too much today," she said, then tapped the letter on top. "But this one looks pretty official."

Jessie took the mail. The return address on the letter said County Courthouse, and there was an official-looking seal stamped below marked Urgent. "We were just about to go inside for lunch," she said. "We'll make sure Grandfather sees this."

"You picked a good time to go inside," Ms. Singleton said, pointing to the eastern sky. An enormous gray cloud was moving in. Soon it would cover the sun and bring a soaking spring rain. "I'd say that's a bad sign."

"Yikes!" Henry said. "Might be a good afternoon for reading a book."

The children waved good-bye to Ms. Singleton. "I wonder why she said that the cloud was a bad sign," Violet said. "A cloud is just a cloud...isn't it?"

Inside, Jessie ran straight to Grandfather's study, with the letter in her hand. Seeing the words about the courthouse had made her nervous. "This just came for you, Grandfather," Jessie said. "You aren't in trouble, are you?"

Grandfather took the letter and chuckled. "I sure hope not," he said. "How about I open it at the table?"

He and the children washed up for lunch, and Mrs. McGregor carried a platter of turkey sandwiches and a fruit salad to the table. Henry poured lemonade, and they all sat down.

Grandfather put on his reading glasses, opened the envelope, and scanned the letter. After a moment, he grinned. "Well, would you look at that."

"It's not trouble, then?" Jessie asked.

Grandfather shook his head. "Nothing to worry about, but it *is* important. This is an official jury summons."

"What's that?" Violet asked.

Grandfather took off his glasses. "Every citizen in our country who is over the age of eighteen has a responsibility to serve on a jury when he or she is called. A jury is just a group of regular people who play an important role in court cases. They listen to the facts and make a decision about whether someone who has been accused of a crime is guilty."

"Wow," Henry said. "That sounds like a big job."

"It can be," Grandfather said. "But I have never done it before. Even as old as I am, I've never been called for jury duty. My friend Sam, on the other hand—that young man who owns the car wash downtown—he just told me last week that he's been called five different times!"

Violet popped a strawberry into her mouth. "Why do they keep calling him instead of you?" she asked.

"They aren't doing it on purpose," Grandfather said. "People are chosen for jury duty at random. So it's just a coincidence that he has been called so many times."

Benny's forehead wrinkled, and he twisted up his mouth. Jessie could tell that he was confused.

"Benny," Jessie said, "a coincidence means something that happens by chance, not for any reason. The people in charge didn't call Sam so many times on purpose."

"Hmm," Benny said. "Well, either way, jury duty sounds pretty boring if you have to sit in a room and listen to a lot of people talk. Unless they have snacks."

Grandfather laughed. "Actually, they do sometimes, if the case goes on a long time. The judge makes sure the jury gets to take breaks for meals, and sometimes they even order food for the jurors to eat if they can't leave the courthouse."

"Like pizza?" Benny asked, his eyes brightening.

"Probably," Grandfather said. "But even without pizza, I am happy to do my duty now that it's my turn. I have to go to Silver City to do it."

"I love Silver City!" Jessie said.

"Yes, me too," said Grandfather, "and come to think of it, this jury summons might be a *good* coincidence. I've been looking for an opportunity to get to Silver City to visit my friend Gwen. We went to high school together, but I haven't seen her in years. She has been going through a bad few months. This could be excellent timing."

Violet looked concerned. "What happened to her?"

"There was a fire in the apartment building Gwen owns—the Bixby," Grandfather said. "Fortunately, no one got hurt. But the building was damaged. It's almost one hundred years old, and it's built in a style called art deco, which was popular in the 1920s."

"What's art deco?" Henry asked, taking the last bite of his sandwich.

"That means the design contains all kinds of interesting decoration," Grandfather said, "like silver and gold and tiles in bright patterns. The whole building is a work of art. It's going to take a lot of careful work to bring it all back to the way it used to be."

"Maybe we could help," Henry said.

Grandfather thought this over. "I'm not sure," he said. "That kind of work can be really difficult. Lots of dirt. Lots of heavy lifting."

"But Grandfather, you saw how much work we did in the front yard today," Jessie said.

"That's right," Henry added. "The Aldens don't shy away from hard work. I think we could handle this job. And don't forget, school is closed on Monday and Tuesday."

Grandfather smiled. "You know, you're right. I would love to introduce you to Gwen, and she sure could use a few extra sets of hands. Let's take a long weekend in Silver City."

Violet clapped her hands. She remembered that she had a book in her room about architecture. She wanted to look in the index to see if it said anything about the art deco style Grandfather had described. It sounded beautiful.

Just then, a large clap of thunder interrupted the conversation, and fat drops began to plink against the window.

"Oh no," Benny said. "The bad sign! Just like Ms. Singleton said."

"Or," Henry said, "it is just a coincidence."

Check out the
Boxcar Children
Interactive Mysteries!

Have you ever wanted to help the Aldens crack a case? Now you can with these interactive, choose-your-path-style mysteries!

978-0-8075-2850-1 · US $6.99

978-0-8075-2860-0 · US $6.99

GERTRUDE CHANDLER WARNER discovered when she was teaching that many readers who like an exciting story could find no books that were both easy and fun to read. She decided to try to meet this need, and her first book, *The Boxcar Children*, quickly proved she had succeeded.

Miss Warner drew on her own experiences to write the mystery. As a child she spent hours watching trains go by on the tracks opposite her family home. She often dreamed about what it would be like to set up housekeeping in a caboose or freight car—the situation the Alden children find themselves in.

While the mystery element is central to each of Miss Warner's books, she never thought of them as strictly juvenile mysteries. She liked to stress the Aldens' independence and resourcefulness and their solid New England devotion to using up and making do. The Aldens go about most of their adventures with as little adult supervision as possible— something else that delights young readers.

Miss Warner lived in Putnam, Connecticut, until her death in 1979. During her lifetime, she received hundreds of letters from girls and boys telling her how much they liked her books.